Artesian Press

MW01045807

THE
PHANTOM
FALCON

ANNE SCHRAFF

Artesian Press

P.O. Box 355 Buena Park, CA 90621

Take Ten Books
Sports

Other Take Ten Themes:
Mystery
Adventure
Disaster
Chillers
Thrillers
Fantasy

Project Editor: Liz Parker
Assistant Editor: Carol Newell
Cover/Text Illustrator: Fujiko
Cover Designer: Tony Amaro
©2001 Artesian Press

ISBN 1-58659-031-6

Chapter 1

Kevin got pumped up just remembering last year when the Lincoln Falcons killed the Cougar's chance for their third soccer championship. Nobody expected much from Kevin Jordan, except maybe his dad, a big soccer fan from his own teen years.

It was two minutes into overtime when a Falcon smashed a shot from the right side. Big, tough Gregg Leeds from the Cougars grinned and blocked it. The Cougars could taste victory, and Gregg would be the hero. But then the ball was kicked to Kevin, and nobody expected Kevin to try to make the goal. Kevin's dad was jumping up and down on his one leg and screaming. Kevin kicked the ball way up into the left-hand corner of the net. The Cougars were beaten.

Kevin would never forget the look he got from Gregg. All of the Falcons were grabbing at Kevin and lifting him off his feet, but all Kevin could remember was the pure hatred in Gregg's eyes.

"You little termite," Gregg hissed later, "wait 'til next year. I'll get a piece of you, you little creep."

This year the two schools were moving towards another showdown. In the first game of the season Kevin and Gregg clashed in an ugly scene. Kevin got a savage elbow in the neck, and for a second he thought his windpipe was busted. Gregg sneered and said, "Go and be a cry baby!"

Kevin didn't complain. He figured he'd get even with a score, and he did. The Falcons won a close one. Gregg would *really* be gunning for Kevin in the next game, but Kevin couldn't let that stop him. It wasn't only for himself that he wanted to win big in soccer—it was also for his dad.

Ever since Kevin was a little kid, he remembered those two pictures on Dad's bedroom wall. One was of Dad at seventeen, winning his high school's soccer championship. The other was an autographed picture of Pele, the Brazilian soccer great.

"When I was about ten, I wanted to be another Pele," Dad often said with a smile. But Vietnam changed all that. At eighteen Kevin's dad lost his right leg to a rocket propelled grenade fired at his helicopter, or his chopper. He came home to become a good mechanic, but the lost dream left a sadness in him. The sadness only seemed to lift completely when Kevin scored in a soccer game.

Now Kevin's bedroom door opened

and there stood Dad. "What're you doing inside on a nice day like this, Kevin?"

"Had to read a story for English, Dad. Test tomorrow. Ms. Finch is tough."

"You've got to keep those grades up, sure," Dad said, winking. "Otherwise there's no chance of Olympic gold or getting to a World Cup match." He winked again and returned to the kitchen for a cup of coffee.

Kevin closed his English book and went outside. At about this time every day Teri Sims came biking by. She was in two of Kevin's classes, and he liked her a lot. But she didn't show much interest in him.

"Hi, Teri," Kevin shouted when she stopped at the sign on the corner.

"Hi, Kevin," she answered. "Have you seen Ricky around?"

Kevin stiffened. Ricky Hall was the star quarterback on Lincoln's football team. All of the girls flocked around him, including Teri. It seemed girls preferred football heroes to soccer stars! Sometimes Kevin wondered if he'd picked the wrong sport. He wasn't really big like most guys who went out for football, but some smaller guys made the team, too.

"I haven't seen him" Kevin muttered. "Hey, Teri, want to go down to the corner for a barbecued sandwich?"

"No, thanks," Teri said, pedaling away.

Kevin stuck his hands in the pockets of his jacket. He loved soccer ever since he was a little kid. But sometimes the pressure got to him. Dad had *such* big dreams, and then there was Gregg's brooding hatred … and always the *next big game*!

Chapter 2

The next day Kevin felt he did okay on the English test. He and his best friend Hollis Jones probably got B's.

"You know, Hollis," Kevin griped at lunch as he wolfed down a baloney sandwich, "being a soccer player doesn't make you popular here."

Hollis laughed and peered through his thick glasses, "Being a guy always getting the best grade in the class makes you downright *unpopular*. Guys from the neighborhood call me crazy."

"Yeah, they quit school in ninth grade. They're the crazy ones. But we're both a couple of freaks," Kevin said bitterly. "I wanted to buy Teri a sandwich yesterday afternoon, and she iced me off."

"I asked Deona to the jazz concert, and she said I'm as exciting as geometry," Hollis said.

"I wonder if I should just forget soccer and build up my muscles for football," Kevin said.

"And break your father's heart? He's been after you for years to bring home that Olympic gold that he got cheated out of, right?" Hollis said.

"Yeah, but come on. I'm good, but …"

Hollis grinned, "Man, nobody's ever gonna forget when you kicked that ball, and it whizzed right into outer space. That Gregg Leeds looked like he'd just had a gold cup snatched out of his hands!"

"Yeah, that's another thing," Kevin said. "Gregg is out to get my hide."

Hollis whistled, "You really can control a game, Kev. It's downright inspiring. In that last game you had the diving save that gave us the win."

"You sound like my Dad! He's already making a space on the mantel for all my trophies!" Kevin said, tossing his brown bag in the trash. Just then Ricky came along with Teri. Teri wore a brand new yellow sweater, and she looked like she belonged on the cover of a magazine.

"Hi, little guy," Ricky said.

Kevin felt his face on fire. Ricky loved to put guys down, especially when there was a cute girl on his arm.

"Oh, Ricky," Teri giggled, "don't insult Kevin. He's not so small. Anyway, all of the soccer players are that way."

Ricky laughed. "Yeah," he said, "all you guys on the soccer team look like you never eat the right breakfast flakes or something."

Kevin stood up, and it turned out that Ricky wasn't that much taller, but he was a lot wider. "Tell me, Ricky, what happened to your neck? Did you ever have a real neck, or were your shoulders always around your ears?"

"Hey, hey," Ricky laughed, "he can give as good as he gets. Well, like we football players always say, the littler they are, the funnier they look!"

Teri covered her mouth with her hands and shook with laughter. Then she hurried off with Ricky.

"Man, she's stuck to him like cotton candy on a kid's mouth," Kevin said. "I'm a big fool ever to have given that girl a look. Why do I need a girl like her who has no brains?"

Kevin was walking home when an old, green sedan slowed down beside him. He only noticed it when he felt the pop bottle, thrown from the car, whiz past his cheek.

"Hey!" Kevin snapped, turning.

Gregg Leeds leaned out the window and said, "Pressure on? I hear that the Falcons are sweating about the big game."

Chapter 3

Kevin was talking to his mother after supper about his bad feelings. "Sometimes I feel like everything is building up in me, like I'm a volcano getting ready to explode."

"Honey, don't do anything if you've stopped enjoying it—like soccer. Don't let your dad make his dreams your own. Nobody can make somebody else's dreams come true," Mom said.

"But I do like soccer. Man, I love the game. And the guys—they're great. We're like brothers. When soccer season is coming on, I'm always up for it. It's fun," Kevin said.

"Then what's the problem, honey?" Mom said, staring at Kevin with her big brown eyes.

"I don't know. There's this stupid girl—no, she's not a stupid girl. She's a nice girl, and I like her. But she has this hero worship for a creepy quarterback."

Mom laughed. "You would give up the sport you love for a sport you don't even like for some girl? Come on, you have more sense than that!"

Kevin laughed. "You're right, Mom. You usually are."

On Saturday Kevin went over to school to practice his kicking game. The game with the Cougars was a week off, and more practice never hurt. A couple of the other guys on the team promised to join him, but as he walked up to the soccer field, he saw only a stranger. Like Kevin he wore a sleeveless shirt and shorts, and he was dark, with a round face.

"Hi," Kevin said.

"Hi," the other guy answered. He

looked a little older than Kevin.

"You a soccer player?" Kevin asked.

"No. I'm a sprinter. My specialty is four hundred yards," he said.

"I've done a little running," Kevin said. "I think it has made my legs stronger for soccer. What's your name?"

"They call me Porkchop," said the boy.

"I'm Kevin. You have a funny nickname. You like porkchops?" Kevin asked.

"Not all that much. My nickname has a long, boring story behind it. Don't expect you got time to hear it. You want to be practicing for the big game Friday," Porkchop said.

"You know about the soccer game with the Cougars?" Kevin asked in surprise.

"Sure. It's a big thing. You know, when I'd run in a big meet I learned something. Motivation was the thing. You just turn off all the distractions.

You just tell yourself there's nothing but that track. In your case, nothing but you and that goal. You just kick for all you're worth and don't let anything get in your way," Porkchop spoke like he knew what he was talking about. That really surprised Kevin. How could a guy not much older than himself have so many smarts?

"You been around, eh, Porkchop?" Kevin said.

"Once or twice," Porkchop said.

"There's this guy with the Cougars, Gregg Leeds. He's sworn he's gonna put me in the hospital. He really takes it personally that my play cheated his team out of the championship last year." Kevin said.

"Are you scared?" Porkchop asked.

If anybody else had asked Kevin that question, he would have been defensive. He probably would have lied and said, "Me scared? No way!" But there was something very real and honest about Porkchop, so Kevin said, "Yeah, some."

"Don't be. Gregg Leeds is a big coward. He talks big, but he won't risk doing you any harm. You got a right foot that's so powerful you can kick your way into the Olympic gold if you want to. When the big night comes, you pretend that Gregg Leeds is no more than paint on the scoreboard. Put that right foot to work and look out!" He finished with a chuckling kind of laugh. He reached out and threw a friendly arm around Kevin's shoulders for a moment, then he walked away.

Kevin was still staring at the space he'd left when the other guys arrived to practice.

"Let's play soccer," Jimmy Hoover shouted.

"Yeah!" Kevin agreed with a strange new enthusiasm.

Chapter 4

The Friday game was on the Cougars' home field, and they had a lot more fans there. Lincoln sent about fifty kids and parents. But all during the game the biggest noise would come from the Cougar fans. Kevin was determined to ignore that. He spotted his Dad ready to start cheering the minute Kevin got a foot on the ball. But there was also a surprise face among the Falcon fans. There sat Teri with a big smile on her face. Kevin met her gaze, and she blew him a kiss!

"Whoa!" Kevin whistled to himself.

With play underway for just two minutes Kevin looked right past Gregg's icy stare and went on a quick scoring binge. He kicked two goals, and the Falcon cheering section went wild. Even Teri was on her feet yelling "Go, Kevin, go!" An ear-to-ear grin split Kevin's face. Winning never felt so good.

Midway through the game Gregg forced Jimmy Hoover to shoot wide, and Jimmy missed a goal. Falcon Coach Ramsey frowned at Jimmy as the Cougar fans stamped their feet in glee. The Cougars scored twice, once with Gregg and once with a giraffe-like forward who pounced on a loose ball.

"We're rolling now," Gregg sneered when he got near Kevin. The score was tied as Kevin sent the ball through the air like a rocket, rippling the net. Kevin had a marvelous feeling that some force was with him, something made him unstoppable.

With two minutes to go in the last half, the score was tied by Gregg's stunning firepower. The last thing the

Falcons needed was a foul, but Jervis Tatum tripped a Cougar and was given a foul. Smelling victory in the air, the Cougars scored. The game was over.

Kevin felt really sorry for Jervis, and he tried to console him. But the other boy wouldn't listen. "I blew it!" he yelled.

"There'll be another game," Kevin said. "The Falcons and the Cougars have the best records in the league. We'll meet for the championship now."

"Yeah!" Gregg said, overhearing the comment. "It's payback time for that championship you stole from us last year."

"We'll see," Kevin snapped, his voice drowned out by the shouting, stomping Cougar fans.

After the game Kevin looked for Teri, but he couldn't find her. He went to the car where his Dad waited. It was a special car for a disabled veteran— one that allowed him to push the pedals with his left leg.

"You were fantastic, Kevin. Too bad those jerks lost it for you," Dad said.

"They aren't jerks, Dad. Jimmy and Jervis are good guys. They're my friends. Everybody has a bad day sometimes."

"Yeah, but they better get their act together when we play the championship, Kevin," Dad said, his face still flushed with excitement from the game.

Kevin did a double take on his dad. He was more pumped up than Kevin was! And he talked about when *we* play the championship game. We? Dad was always looking ahead to World Cup competition and the Olympics. It was like a big boulder rested on Kevin's shoulders. Sure, Kevin loved soccer, but he wanted it to be a game. Kevin wasn't ready to make soccer his life! He had a whole other life planned. He loved English, and he wanted to work for a newspaper or a television station as a reporter.

Kevin wanted to say, "Dad, give me a break! I'm not Pele! I'll never be Pele!" But when Kevin opened his mouth to say the words, they stuck in his throat. His dad was grinning, reliving Kevin's plays, busting with pride.

Chapter 5

Teri cornered Kevin at school and told him what a great soccer game he played. Then she said, "I'm really worried about that English paper in Ms. Finch's class. You're so smart, Kevin. Could you help me get my notes together?"

"Sure," Kevin said eagerly. A chance to spend time with Teri wasn't something he'd turn down.

"Oh, great. I'll bring what I have over to your house after school. Then after we get organized, maybe we could go out for two of those barbecued sandwiches you've been talking so much about."

"All right!" Kevin said.

Teri was wearing a pink pullover sweater and jeans when she came to Kevin's house. She held a few scraps of paper in her hand. Those were her notes.

Ms. Finch wanted the students to choose two major American fiction writers and compare their styles. The paper counted for forty percent of the grade for the semester. Kevin had chosen Ernest Hemingway and F. Scott Fitzgerald, and his paper was already finished.

"I just jotted down a few things," Teri said. "I'm comparing some guy named Herbert Melvin with Edgar Allan Roe. He's the guy who wrote all that horror stuff."

Kevin was shocked at how confused Teri was. She was a smart girl but kind of lazy. She never did her homework. "Their names are Herman Melville and Edgar Allan Poe," he said gently.

"Whatever," Teri said with a shrug.

"Well, what I have already is that Melvin, or Melville, wrote about fish in *Moby Dick,* and Poe wrote about birds, like in 'The Raven.'"

"Well," Kevin said, "the main difference between these two guys is …"

"It's very confusing to me," Teri said, going to the refrigerator for a cola. After an hour and a half Kevin had written five pages of notes, and Teri had finished two colas and some ice cream.

They took a break and got some barbecued sandwiches. Teri kept telling Kevin how smart he was and how grateful she was for all his work.

As Kevin walked Teri home, he handed her the notes he'd written. "You can check this over and add some more stuff, then just type it up. You should be okay, Teri."

"You're a real doll, Kevin," she said.

At Teri's house Kevin got a pleasant surprise. She put her hands on his shoulders and kissed him.

All the way home Kevin felt higher than when he'd kicked two soccer goals in a row. But deep down he had a nagging doubt. Would tonight have happened if Teri didn't need help on her English paper?

"Hi, honey," Mom called when Kevin came in. "Did you get Teri home okay?"

"Yeah."

Mom stood in the doorway. "That's nice helping another student with her work, Kevin, but it sounded like you were doing it all," she said.

"Oh, no," Kevin lied, "I was explaining it to her. She understands it all now. She just needed a little help. Now she's gonna add a lot more of her own ideas and type up the paper."

"Well, that's good," Mom said. "because if you do all the work, you're just cheating. She's the one getting cheated!"

Chapter 6

Kevin was disappointed at school the next day when Teri was hanging out with Ricky again. It was like nothing had happened last night.

"I'll tell you what," Hollis explained at lunch, "Girls are like summer. You look forward to it every year, and you just end up with mosquito bites and sweat."

But then, the next afternoon before soccer practice, Teri appeared at the end of the field. "Oh, Kevin, I'm in big trouble! I'm doomed," Teri groaned.

"What's the matter?" Kevin asked.

"That paper is due tomorrow, and I haven't typed it up! Mom was going to type it tonight, but she has to work at the hospital. If I don't turn it in tomorrow morning, Ms. Finch will flunk me!" Teri wailed.

"Can't you type it up, Teri?"

"I'm a terrible typist. It'll look so sloppy. Oh, Kevin, would you be an angel and type it for me? You got an A in typing."

Kevin felt anger rising in him. Coach Ramsey was yelling, "Are you getting in the game or not? If you don't have time for practice, maybe you shouldn't be playing soccer!"

"Kevin, my Dad'll whip me if I flunk English," Teri cried, her voice shaking.

"Oh, okay," Kevin said, grabbing the packet of notes and stuffing them in his backpack. Then he trotted over to take his position for soccer practice.

Coach Ramsey snarled, "Now maybe we can get a little action back into this bumbling bunch of losers!" Coach Ramsey was really ticked off since the loss to the Cougars.

Late that night Kevin's dad came in as Kevin was typing Teri's paper. "What's that you're doing, son?"

"English paper," Kevin muttered.

"You usually don't leave stuff for the last minute," Dad said.

Kevin grunted. He was ashamed to admit he was typing another student's paper. He was more ashamed when he found out Teri had added nothing to the notes he wrote. So Kevin had done all the research and now he was typing her paper. He was a cheat, and it bothered him. He felt like he'd just taken a swim in a polluted lake. "Coach Ramsey's been driving us hard. He wants us really sharp for the championship game," Kevin said. "I let some school stuff slip."

"Coach doesn't have any complaints about your performance, Kevin. You were something to see in that last game."

"Yeah," Kevin muttered. He ripped the last page out of the typewriter.

"You played the whole game with intensity. Some of the guys were goofing off. Anybody could see that. Not you. You've got the concentration of a champ. I was like that, Kevin. I still remember that game where my school got the big one. The trophy. It's still there at Adams High with our names on it." Dad's voice trailed off, and he got a sad, faraway look in his eye.

Kevin had heard the story of his dad's big game a hundred times. But, strangely, Dad never went into any details on the day he lost his leg in Vietnam. All Kevin knew was that his dad had taken another guy's place that day because the other pilot was sick. If not for that quirk of fate, Kevin's dad might have gone on to be a soccer great.

Kevin wished that his dad had been able to play in the World Cup and maybe gone to the Olympics. Then he would have lived his own dream.

Then the burden wouldn't be on Kevin's shoulders to live a dream that didn't start in his own heart—a dream that showed signs of becoming a nightmare.

Chapter 7

"Do you have it?" Teri asked when Kevin arrived at school.

"Yeah, here," Kevin almost snapped, "but I don't feel right about doing it for you. I'm just cheating you."

"Aww, Kevin, I'll read it over and learn a lot. Oh, Kev, let's do something really special together this weekend, okay?"

"Because you want to Teri, or because you think you owe me? Because you don't owe me," Kevin said.

"Kevin, don't be like that," Teri said, reaching up and stroking his cheek with her soft hand. "I really, really like you. You're terrific."

"Okay," Kevin saïd, a smile breaking through his frown. "We'll go see a movie and get some good pizza."

"Kevin, that sounds wonderful!" Teri said before she hurried off.

It was hard to keep his mind on soccer practice with the weekend coming up, but Kevin didn't miss any of it. He really wanted to win the championship for Lincoln—it wasn't just for Dad. Coach Ramsey never had a championship team, and though he was a crusty old grouch, he really loved the guys. Soccer was what had kept some of them out of trouble. Coach was always there to hash out a boy's problems. Kevin liked his teammates, too. So Kevin put his heart into every practice session even though Teri was in his heart through it all.

Kevin took Teri to a movie he thought she'd enjoy—a drama about relationships. He would have rather seen a horror movie about an acid dripping monster, but he figured it was all about

Teri having a good time. That's what he wanted most. They got pizza afterwards and ate it under a tree in the park.

"I had the best time ever," Teri said.

"Me, too," Kevin said. His heart started pounding when she kissed him a couple of times. He felt like the school band was marching inside his chest.

At school on Monday Kevin was still thinking about the date. He kept looking for chances to see Teri and wave or smile to make sure she still liked him. Teri smiled and even blew him a kiss once. But she had pom-pom practice at lunch, so they couldn't eat together like Kevin planned. Kevin ended up eating with Hollis as usual.

"So it's going good for you and the girl, huh?" Hollis asked.

"Yeah!" Kevin said, grinning.

Just then Deona Wallace strolled over. She looked right at Kevin and said, "Poor baby."

"What's that supposed to mean?" Kevin asked.

"Teri is telling everybody she had the worst date of her entire life on Sunday with some boring soccer player. She said she had to sit through a totally stupid movie and then eat a stale pizza in the park, chasing flies away!"

Hollis broke in. "Deona was just born mean. She *always* gets up on the wrong side of the bed, and all day she walks around trying to cause trouble."

"I don't believe Teri would say stuff like that," Kevin said, glaring at Deona.

Deona laughed. "You believe anything you want. Guys are all totally stupid, anyway. They never take a second look at a girl who isn't a cheerleader. Girls like Teri play you for fools, and it's nothing more than you got coming to you!" With that, Deona marched away.

Kevin hurled half his remaining

sandwich in the trash. He stuck his hands in the pockets of his jacket. Sure, Deona was a mean spirited girl. No surprise there. But she wasn't a liar. What she said had the painful ring of truth to it.

Chapter 8

Kevin felt like dumping everything, even the Falcons. He was sick of everybody using him for their own reasons. On his way home from school he ran into Teri. He thought about screaming at her for what she'd done, but then he had too much pride for that. He wouldn't let her know how much she'd hurt him.

"Ms. Finch really seemed to like my paper, Kevin." Teri said sweetly. "I'm just so grateful that you helped me."

Kevin forced a smile to his face. "I'm glad it did you some good, but I won't be doing anything like that again. It's not fair to you, okay? And it makes me feel like a cheater. Anyway, I gotta

go." He turned and jogged off towards home. He had to pass the soccer field as he ran. They were practicing, but he wouldn't be going, not today. Coach Ramsey could yell his head off, Kevin didn't care.

Kevin heard the familiar voice as he passed the soccer field. "Hey! Jordan!"

Kevin didn't even turn his head. He just turned up the volume on his tape player and let the music blast his brain.

He didn't expect Ramsey to bounce through the fence and plant himself in Kevin's path. "Take those headphones off!" he ordered. "I need to talk to you."

Kevin took off the headphones and stared at the man. "I'm getting sick of soccer," Kevin almost shouted. "Practice, practice, practice, like we're getting ready for doomsday or something."

"What are you saying to me? Don't you enjoy the game anymore, Kevin?" Coach Ramsey asked in a softer voice.

The blue eyes looked concerned. Ramsey could turn from raging bull to caring old bear in a split second.

"Well, my dad loves soccer. He figures I'm going to bring home Olympic gold one day or be in the World Cup, and that's crazy! Soccer used to be fun, but now it's life or death, and I hate that," Kevin said.

"I hate it, too, Kevin. It's a fun game for kids, period. I get mad when you guys don't do your best. I also get mad in my history class when kids get careless and mix up World War I with World War II. But I'll still love you guys if you lose the bloody championship." A twinkle came to Coach Ramsey's eyes. "Is that *all* that's bugging you today, Jordan?"

"No," Kevin admitted, grinning a little, too. "Some girl played me for a fool. She got me to do something that wasn't right just to get on her good side. Turns out her good side isn't worth being on."

Coach Ramsey laughed. "Well, you learned a good lesson, Jordan. Everybody has to learn those kinds of lessons. The younger you are when you learn them, the less it hurts."

Kevin glanced across the soccer field at his teammates. There was a lump in Kevin's throat when he saw the clump of blue uniforms, the white knee socks, the shirts with the soaring falcon on the front and the number on the back.

"Kevin," Coach Ramsey said, "it's not going to be easy, but you have to find the courage to tell your dad his dream is not your dream. It'll probably take a lot more guts than facing the Cougars—even Gregg Leeds' killer eyes and dynamite foot. But you've got to do it."

"Yeah," Kevin agreed.

"What do you want to do now, son?" Coach Ramsey asked. "Suit up or go home?"

Kevin sighed, then he smiled. "Suit up," he said.

Chapter 9

It was a week before the championship game, and Kevin and his dad were watching TV. Dad was in a good mood, eating popcorn, and laughing at the stale jokes on the show. Kevin figured if he was ever going to come clean with his dad about soccer, now was the time.

"Soccer is a lot of fun for me, Dad," he said.

"I know, Kevin. It was for me too when I was a kid," Dad said.

"I mean playing, not just winning," Kevin said nervously.

"Sure, but every athlete wants to win, right?" Dad said.

"Not always," Kevin said. His mouth was dry. He felt shaky. Coach

Ramsey was right. This was *much* tougher than jostling shoulders with Gregg Leeds over a soccer ball. "You know, Dad, I'll always want to, you know, play soccer, but, uh, not big time. I mean, I'll play with the guys for fun, or maybe coach a team, or just kick the ball around with the neighborhood kids ..."

Dad had stopped smiling. He'd stopped eating popcorn. He was staring at Kevin in silence. That made it even tougher.

"Dad, it's just that I don't think I want to play soccer after I get out of school, you know, in competition and stuff. I just want to do it for fun," Kevin struggled with each word.

Dad's eyes widened. "How long have you felt this way, Kevin?" he finally asked.

"Always, I guess."

"When I'd talk about 'my young Pele' and making the Olympic team or maybe turning pro, why didn't you ever say anything?" Dad asked.

Suddenly he looked old and sad. He looked like something precious had been stolen from him—maybe the most precious thing in his whole life. His dream died once in Vietnam. Then it came back to life in Kevin's talent. Now it had been killed again.

Kevin hung his head. "I'm sorry, Dad," he whispered.

"No, no, it's okay," Dad said as he got up. "It's your life." He seemed to wobble more when he stood. He walked to his bedroom and closed the door heavily.

Kevin groaned, "Congratulations! You just busted your old man's heart!"

Kevin got the idea over the next few days that his father wouldn't be coming to the championship game. It would be the first time he ever missed a game. It tore Kevin's heart to think about it.

"I wish Dad would come to the

game," Kevin told his mother when he came home from the final practice session.

"Well, your Dad has been feeling a little tired," Mom said, but she was only pretending. She knew what had happened as well as Kevin did.

"Mom, try to get him to come, okay?" Kevin almost begged. Mom just shrugged like it was probably a lost cause.

That night Kevin turned it over in his own mind whether he should play in the championship game. It would be a dirty trick on his teammates and on Coach Ramsey to turn up sick, but Kevin lacked the heart to play.

As Kevin thought about it, a strange thing happened. Porkchop seemed to be there again in the darkness of his bedroom. He wasn't really there, but his words seemed to ring in the air with the clarity of a bell.

"You just kick for all you're worth,

and don't let anything get in your way."

Kevin blinked. Suddenly he knew he'd play no matter how he felt. He had to play. He'd given his word and a lot of people were depending on him. He'd have to play for his own self respect.

And Kevin knew something else, too. The championship game would be the most important game he ever played—win or lose.

Chapter 10

There were only seconds to kickoff, and no sign of Kevin's dad. Kevin's mind leaped back to his first soccer summer camp, and he got a lump in his throat. Soccer had always been such fun—until now!

With the game underway for two minutes, Tommy Wilson, a Cougar, spun the ball around the Falcon defenders for a score. Everybody in the Cougar cheering section went wild. Kevin took another glance into the stands. His heart almost stopped. Dad! He waved to Kevin, grinned, and sat down. Kevin's spirits soared.

The Falcons had the ball, but it was intercepted at mid-field. Kevin was pushed down from behind by a sneer-ing Gregg. He was banged down hard, but a foul wasn't called. Gregg winked as if he had it all going his way. He scored in the next second. It was 2-0 for the Cougars mid-way through the first half.

The Cougars kept up their steam. Kevin tried desperately to get off a shot, but Gregg was shadowing him, staying tight with him and blocking. All of the Cougars were playing fierce de-fense.

Then, suddenly, Kevin saw him— Porkchop! He was wearing Falcon blue, and he seemed to clear a spot for Kevin's kick. Kevin blinked in astonish-ment and made a powerful right foot kick, hurling the ball like a rocket. The Cougars never saw the speeding ball until it was in the net. The score went 2-1 with the Cougars still leading.

Kevin fired again but the shot was kicked away. The loose ball bounced near the corner. Kevin found the ball coming his way in mid-field and he kicked, but again it was intercepted. Jimmy Hoover scored then with an assist from Kevin. The score was tied 2-2.

Coach Ramsey got the boys together for a half-time pep talk. "You can do it. Just don't get too tense!"

At the kickoff for the second half Kevin tried to get a shot, but a Cougar kicked it away. The ball sailed out of play. Kevin's next shot went wildly into the stands. He was really feeling the pressure, and Gregg made the most of it, mocking him. Kevin ran a foot race with Gregg and tried again to take the ball. Gregg got it instead, scoring. The score went to 3-2, Cougars.

The Cougars offensive pressure was white hot. They really wanted this championship. Kevin looked for a chance to score, but Gregg kept riding his back. Partway through the second half the score still favored the Cougars, 3-2.

It was do or die in the final minutes of the game. Kevin found the ball smothered by Cougar defensive plays. He felt a sharp elbow to his head. It was another of Gregg's dirty tricks, and he got away with it. No foul was called.

Kevin kicked the ball, but again it was blocked. The minutes ticking away were his enemy now. The Falcons regrouped in mid-field, trying to get around the Cougar defense. Kevin's heart was pounding madly. The Cougars were playing terrific soccer to defend that one-point lead.

Kevin raced after the ball and kicked with his powerful right foot, his best kick thus far in the game. It sailed into the net for a score. It went right through a Cougar's legs! Now the score was tied 3-3.

With sixty seconds left in the game

Kevin tried to put across the winning goal. The ball was in mid-field when he made a fantastic long kick, sending the ball smashing into the net. That was the game. The Cougars never came back as the Falcon fans exploded in celebration.

Kevin went into the stands and hugged his dad, who had tears in his eyes. Later Kevin would give his dad the championship trophy to hold for the pictures. "I'm so glad you came, Dad," Kevin said. "It made all the difference."

"I almost didn't," Dad admitted. "But a weird thing happened. I saw this guy—the one whose place I took in Vietnam—it was sorta like a dream. He always felt guilty that I lost my leg taking *his* place that day. Well, he says to me, 'Go to that game, Tom Jordan'. So I came. The really creepy part is that the guy has been dead for twenty years!"

Kevin felt numb. "What was the

guy's name Dad?" he asked.

Dad smiled. "He had this round face and he was a great chopper pilot ... so we called him Porkchop."